THE ADVENTURES OF
Sir Gawain the TRUE

THE KNIGHTS' TALES

THE ADVENTURES OF

Sir Gawain the TRUE

GERALD MORRIS

ILLUSTRATED BY

AARON RENIER

HOUGHTON MIFFLIN
HOUGHTON MIFFLIN HARCOURT
BOSTON NEW YORK 2011

Houghton Mifflin is an imprint of
Houghton Mifflin Harcourt Publishing Company.

www.hmhbooks.com

The text of this book is set in Post Mediaeval.
The illustrations are brush and ink.

Library of Congress Cataloging-in-Publication Control Number
2010006808

Manufactured in the United States
DOC 10 9 8 7 6 5 4 3 2 1
4500285220

FOR JULIAN AND JONTY,

WHO HEARD THIS FIRST.

Contents

Chapter 1
Sir Gawain the Undefeated

Now, everyone who knows anything at all about knights knows that they used to dress in metal suits and bash each other off their horses with pointy sticks called lances. This only makes sense, of course. Anyone who happened to have a metal suit, a horse, and a pointy stick would do the same.

Some may have also heard that knights fought dragons as well, often to rescue damsels. (Damsels are what they used to call women. Don't ask why;

they just did.) This is less sensible, because—Well, really now! What would a dragon want with a damsel? Still, if a dragon did for some reason make off with one, then it would be perfectly reasonable for a knight to rescue her.

But what many do not realize is that, at least in King Arthur's court, knights were also expected to be courteous and respectful. The king was very clear about this: He wanted no bullies at his Round Table. In fact, he said that courtesy was even more important than wearing metal suits and bashing people from horses. Not surprisingly, this notion took a while to sink in. Knights who had spent their whole lives learning swordsmanship and pointy-stick-bashing did not always see how something else could be more important. Indeed, King Arthur had reigned for several years before he felt that his knights were starting to get the idea.

During those early years, the most celebrated of King Arthur's knights was his nephew Sir Gawain. Sir Gawain had won so many tournaments—which is what knights called the contests where they did all that bashing—that he was called Sir Gawain the Undefeated. One day, as Sir Gawain the Undefeated was riding through a forest, he heard a loud scream and a ferocious roar. Sir Gawain urged his horse forward and soon came upon a huge black lizard that was holding a damsel in one scaly, knobby claw.

"Whatever does a dragon want with a damsel?" wondered Sir Gawain. The idea seemed absurd to him as well.

But Sir Gawain did not have time for philosophical questions, because at that moment the dragon roared again, sending a ball of fire into the air, and the damsel screamed. Sir Gawain charged. It was a fierce battle, which took quite a

long time, and an onlooker would doubtless have found it gripping to watch. For some reason, though, secondhand blow-by-blow accounts of battles are not nearly so interesting as the things themselves, so it won't hurt anything to skip ahead here. What matters is that when the fight was over, the dragon lay dead at Sir Gawain's feet.

"Hooray!" shouted Sir Gawain triumphantly. "I won again!"

"Oh, thank you, Sir Knight!" cried the damsel. "You saved my life!"

"Yes, I suppose I did," agreed Sir Gawain. "By the way, do you have any idea why the dragon captured you?"

"What difference does that make?" the damsel replied. "He was an evil creature."

"Just wondering," Sir Gawain said.

"What matters is that you saved me, Sir Knight," the damsel repeated.

"Not Sir Knight," Sir Gawain corrected. "I'm Sir Gawain. Sir Gawain the Undefeated."

"I'm ever so grateful to you, Sir Gawain."

"Yes, I suppose you are," Sir Gawain replied. He turned back to the dragon's corpse and gazed at it with satisfaction. "It was quite a fight, wasn't it? Did you see how the lizard tried to get behind me but I reversed my lance? A very tricky bit of lancemanship, let me tell you!"

"Er, quite," said the damsel.

"And how, when it shifted to my weak side, I tossed my sword to my left hand? Not everyone can do that, you know."

"Very clever of you, I'm sure." The damsel's smile was smaller now. "Sir Gawain, to thank you for your service, I would like to give you a gift: this green sash." The woman began to remove a gleaming strip of green silk from her waist. "Wear this as a reminder of your victory, and—"

"Oh, I shan't forget this victory," Sir Gawain said.

"But this is a special sash. As long as you wear it—"

"I really don't have a place for a sash," Sir Gawain said. "Why don't you keep it?"

"Oh," the damsel said. "Well . . . if you wish. But I want to thank you somehow. Perhaps it would be enough if I gave you a kiss on the cheek, just to—"

"I say!" interrupted Sir Gawain. "You don't think that just because I saved your life we're, you know, *in love* or something, do you?"

"What?"

"Because a lot of girls might think that, but really I would have saved any damsel. It didn't have to be you. Besides, I'm not looking for a lady of my own right now."

"A lady *of your own?*" gasped the damsel. "I never said—"

"Nothing personal, of course," Sir Gawain said hurriedly. "I'm sure you'll make a very nice lady for someone someday. It's just that I'm not in the market for romance at the moment."

"Of all the . . . All I wanted to do was show you my gratitude!"

Suddenly remembering King Arthur's lectures on courtesy, Sir Gawain bowed and said, "You're very welcome," then turned his horse and rode away. He was already thinking about how he would tell the tale of his great victory once he got back to the Round Table.

The story was a success. Sir Gawain held the court spellbound as he recounted his defeat of the horrible dragon, even during the duller bits when he described his lancemanship. But when he told about his conversation with the damsel after the battle, King Arthur sat up.

"Do you mean to say, Gawain," the king asked, "that the lady tried to give you a token of thanks and you refused it?"

"Well, yes."

"So then she asked if she could give you one kiss on the cheek, and you turned that down as well?"

"I didn't want her to get the wrong idea, you see."

"And I gather that you told her your name but never asked for hers?"

Sir Gawain blinked. The king was right. He had no idea who the lady was.

"And then," King Arthur concluded, "you rode away, leaving her alone, on foot, in the forest?"

For a moment, Sir Gawain was silent. "I didn't think about that," he admitted, frowning. "That wasn't . . . wasn't my best choice, was it?"

King Arthur shook his head.

"I *did* say 'You're welcome,'" Sir Gawain said. "'*Very* welcome,' I think."

King Arthur covered his eyes with his hands. Sometimes in those early days he wondered what it would take to prove to his knights that courtesy was as important as courage.

CHAPTER 2

The Green Knight

Several months after Sir Gawain the Undefeated overcame the dragon, the knight faced a new and very different sort of challenge. It happened at King Arthur's Christmas feast.

Now, there may be some who think they've been to Christmas feasts, but the truth is that unless they've been to one of King Arthur's feasts, they really don't know what they're talking about.

Never before or since have there been grander yuletide banquets. King Arthur's feasts lasted for seven days—from Christmas right up to New Year's—and every evening was more magnificent than the evening before. There were so many luscious foods at his feasts that it would be cruel to describe them. King Arthur's cooks were like kitchen magicians. It is said that Brussels sprouts prepared by King Arthur's chefs tasted better than custard pies prepared by anyone else.

Their recipe for Brussels sprouts has, alas, been lost.

But the feast was more than just the food. Every evening there was a different entertainment for the court, each astounding in its own way. One night, the lightest and most agile acrobats ever seen flipped themselves and tossed each other about the banquet hall with uncanny ease. Another evening, a French musician sang ballads of romance, and so touching was his performance that everyone at court fell in love with someone for as long as the music lasted. (Don't worry; they all got better afterward.) There were side-splittingly funny jesters and grippingly suspenseful story-tellers, and on the last night of the feast there performed a famous juggler named Launfal the Light-fingered who was so deft that he could juggle five sleeping cats without waking even one.

It was during Launfal's act that adventure arrived at Camelot. Just as the juggler launched the cats, there came a scream from the kitchen, followed a second later by a deafening crash of breaking dishes. Then the kitchen doors burst open, and into the banquet hall rode a huge knight on a monstrous steed, and both horse and rider were as green as the grass in May.

Ladies screamed and knights leaped to their feet, grabbing for their weapons, which they didn't

actually have, since one doesn't generally arm oneself for a Christmas feast. Launfal the Light-fingered's cats awoke with a chorus of angry squalls and began grabbing with their claws at anything that was near, which was mostly Launfal. The Green Knight stopped in front of King Arthur's table, his fierce eyes gazing, unblinking, about the room. He took a breath and opened his mouth to speak.

"Please excuse me," he said. "I didn't mean to cause such a stir. Am I interrupting?"

"Er, yes," replied the king, rising to his feet, "I suppose you are, a bit. This is our Christmas feast."

"A thousand pardons," said the Green Knight, "but I was looking for King Arthur."

"I am King Arthur."

"Excellent!" the Green Knight exclaimed, dismounting. "I've come to bring you some entertainment."

"Well," said the king, "as it happens, when you arrived we were watching this juggler."

"What, that fellow with the cats in his hair? That's what you call entertainment? It's a good thing I came when I did. I bring a merry little game to amuse—"

But the Green Knight got no further. At that moment rose one of King Arthur's knights, a skilled fighter who had never been overcome by any knight except Sir Gawain and who was called Sir Gandefere the Nearly Undefeated. Sir

Gandefere broke abruptly into the conversation, shouting, "Who do you think you are? You can't just barge into the king's feast like this!" Walking around his table, Sir Gandefere stepped bravely up to the Green Knight. "Why don't you go back where you—?"

Sighing softly, the Green Knight brought his fist down on Sir Gandefere's head, like a hammer. Sir Gandefere crumpled to the floor. The Green Knight said, "Your knights are very brave, O king. But it's rude to speak when someone else is talking, you know. As I was saying, I bring a game, a test of knightly arts. Is there a knight here who would take on a little challenge?"

At once, two knights leaped to their feet: Sir Reynold the Brave and Sir Gawain the Undefeated. "Sire!" they called at once. "Let me! Let me!"

The Green Knight looked at them. "And what are your names, O knights?"

Sir Reynold and Sir Gawain told the Green Knight their names and titles.

The uncanny visitor smiled, showing gleaming light green teeth. "Sir Gawain the Undefeated! Excellent!" he said. "I have heard of you. They say that you can stand before any knight and match him blow for blow."

"So can I!" said Sir Reynold.

"I do my best," murmured Sir Gawain, trying to look modest.

The Green Knight didn't even look at Sir Reynold. "Then you are perfect for my game, Sir Gawain, because that's all you have to do."

"I beg your pardon?" asked Sir Gawain.

"Trade blows," explained the Green Knight. "First you strike me; then I strike you."

Sir Gawain hesitated, glancing at the senseless form of Sir Gandefere lying at the knight's feet.

"Gawain," said King Arthur, "perhaps it would be best not to play this particular game."

"Then let me!" begged Sir Reynold.

"I'm not afraid," announced Sir Gawain. "I've never turned down a challenge, and I won't begin now! I'll play this game with you. I swear it!"

King Arthur frowned, but the strange knight only showed his green smile again. "Then we're agreed," he said. With that he reached behind him and drew a long, wicked axe from his horse's saddle.

"Um, with an axe?" asked Sir Gawain.

"You promised," the Green Knight reminded him, handing him the weapon and kneeling at his feet. "Go on, then. Right on the neck."

Sir Gawain didn't move. "It's just that I was thinking of something less drastic. You know, fisticuffs."

"Do King Arthur's knights keep their vows or not?" the Green Knight demanded.

"I would!" said Sir Reynold, under his breath.

Sir Gawain sighed, then said, "Right, then. Sorry

about this." With a single swift blow, he drove the axe blade down, cutting the Green Knight's head neatly from his shoulders.

Most of the knights and ladies looked away from the sprawled, headless body. King Arthur shook his head slowly. "And he called this a *game?*" he muttered.

"Odd sort of game," Sir Gawain agreed. "I didn't have any fun at all, and as for this fellow, I can't imagine that he enjoyed himself any more than . . ."

Sir Gawain trailed off. At his feet, the Green Knight's body had begun to move. It pushed itself up with its arms, then groped about until it located its detached head. Then, head in hands, the green body rose to its feet. The head's eyes flickered open, and it grinned its green smile.

"Well struck, Sir Gawain," said the head. "Now I get a turn. But no hurry. Shall we say one year from tonight? Next New Year's Day, you meet me at my home. It's called the Green Chapel, and you should have no trouble finding it."

With that, the Green Knight took his axe from Sir Gawain, leaped into his horse's saddle, and rode from the court.

CHAPTER 3
Spinagras the Dwarf

After the Green Knight had gone, the knights and ladies of the court agreed that their New Year's visitor had been a sorcerer. Who but a powerful enchanter could ride away with his head tucked under one arm? Privately, the knights and ladies agreed on something else, too: Sir Gawain, who was *not* a sorcerer and was *not* able to get about with a separated head, was doomed. Consequently, there was great sadness at Camelot.

This sadness included Sir Gawain, of course. He knew better than anyone that when the Green Knight struck his neck, he would not survive. He considered not going to the Green Chapel at all, but only for a moment. He had taken a vow, after all, and Sir Gawain always kept his vows. But he did spend a good deal of time wondering why he had taken such a foolish vow to begin with. For the first time in his life, Sir Gawain wondered if living up to his reputation as "Sir Gawain the Undefeated" was as important as he'd thought.

Only King Arthur refused to give up hope. If one enchanter could survive beheading, then perhaps another enchanter could help Sir Gawain do the same. "We will seek help from Merlin!" he announced. Merlin was the powerful enchanter who had helped Arthur become king.

"But Merlin left England after you were crowned," Gawain pointed out.

"So he did," the king conceded. "But you never

can tell about sorcerers. I haven't said anything to the court, but in recent months reports have come of a powerful enchanter living in the north. Perhaps this is Merlin himself, returned to England. I will go at once to seek his counsel. Who will go with me?"

All the knights of the Round Table said that they would go, and so it was that two days later, the king and his knights set out on the Great North Road. The sky was heavy and gray when the party left, and it grew darker each day they traveled, but the king refused to let the threatening snow delay their journey. When the snow started on the fourth day, though, he began to wonder if he'd been entirely wise. It fell so thickly that the knights could hardly see their hands before their faces. Soon the party was hopelessly lost. The king called for all to dismount and tie ropes between them so that no one got separated

from the rest, which worked perfectly except that nobody thought to tie ropes to the pack horses that carried their supplies. When the snow finally stopped, no one had any idea where they or their supplies were. All they knew was that knights and supplies were no longer together.

"Bother," said King Arthur.

"Maybe there's a town or a castle nearby where we could buy provisions," suggested Sir Gawain.

The king nodded. "Why don't you and Reynold scout around and see what you can find?" The two knights nodded. "And remember," added King Arthur, "*ask.*"

So the two knights set off in opposite directions. Sir Reynold rode west and within an hour came upon a clearing in the forest, where two huge cook fires roared. Over one blaze a whole ox was roasting, and over the other sizzled a gigantic wild boar. On a blanket by the fire were heaped several freshly cooked fowl. "Now *there's* something like!" exclaimed the knight.

"What do you want?" snapped a stern, rather high-pitched voice. Sir Reynold had to look about the clearing twice before he located the speaker, a red-bearded dwarf standing near the ox.

"Some food, of course! I'm starving!"

"Well, you can't have any!" sniffed the dwarf. "This is my food."

"All yours?" demanded Sir Reynold.

"Do you see anyone else here?" retorted the dwarf.

"Don't be ridiculous!" gasped Sir Reynold. "A little fellow like you? You don't need all this!"

"I'm *very* hungry," replied the dwarf. He turned his back on Sir Reynold and began turning the ox on its spit.

"That's the stupidest thing I've ever heard! Why, you'd pop if you ate a tenth of this! I'm having lunch!" With that, Sir Reynold dismounted and lifted a chicken from the stack on the blanket. At once, brilliant green and yellow lights seemed to burst in front of his eyes, and that was the last thing Sir Reynold remembered for some time.

Not long after this, Sir Gawain rode into the dwarf's clearing. Having found nothing to the east, he had circled around, hoping to meet up with Sir Reynold. Like Sir Reynold, Sir Gawain gazed at all the dwarf's food with amazement. "My goodness!" he exclaimed.

"What do you want?" demanded the dwarf's thin voice.

Sir Gawain nodded his head in greeting. "Good afternoon," he said.

The dwarf grunted. "Good afternoon," he replied, grudgingly. "Who are you?"

"My name is Sir Gawain," said Sir Gawain. Then he added, "And what's your name?"

The dwarf's scowl lightened a little bit. "I'm called Spinagras. Now are you going to answer my question? What do you want?"

"I'm traveling with King Arthur, and we were separated from our supplies during the storm. I was scouting for food."

Spinagras nodded slowly, then turned back to the ox. "Well, good luck."

Sir Gawain hesitated. "Er . . . I say, friend Spinagras . . ."

"Yes?"

"*You* seem to have a good deal of food."

"So?"

"I was just wondering if maybe you had enough to share with King Arthur's party."

Spinagras didn't even turn around. "This is *my* food."

"Yes, of course," Sir Gawain replied. "But are you quite sure that you need all of it?"

At last the dwarf turned and gazed challengingly into Sir Gawain's eyes. "What if I said that I did? What would you do then?"

Sir Gawain sighed. The smell of roasting meat was tantalizing, but he only said, "I suppose I'd have to ride on and keep looking."

Spinagras's eyes widened with surprise. "Just ride on? You wouldn't take even a little bit? You could, you know; you're bigger than I am. You could cut off my head in a second."

Sir Gawain shook his head. "I don't think I will, though, if it's all right with you. King Arthur told us if we found someone with food, we were to ask politely. That's all."

"So why haven't you?"

Sir Gawain blinked. Thinking back over their conversation, he realized that he never had actually asked. "Would you share your food with us?"

"Would I share my food with you *what?*"

"Er, please?"

Spinagras smiled broadly. "Well said, Sir Gawain! Go fetch your king and tell him to come to dinner."

"Really?"

"I was just waiting to be asked. You'd be amazed at how rude some passing knights can be. Why, the fellow before you was an absolute lout."

From this description, Sir Gawain guessed he had found Sir Reynold. "And, if I may ask, what happened to that knight?"

"He had an accident, and I sent him off tied to his horse's saddle. He'll be fine, barring a bit of a bump on the head. Well? What are you waiting for? Your king's hungry. I'll start another ox."

So it was that soon afterward, all King Arthur's knights were well fed, and the king had procured supplies for their journey from Spinagras, who, it turned out, was steward of a great estate. Spinagras

assured the king that he would be happy to sup-
ply the king with anything he needed, free of
charge.

"Are you sure?" asked the king. "I'm willing to
pay."

"Don't be silly," replied Spinagras. "Every noble
in England has vowed to support you, sire. Giving
you food is just keeping that vow."

Since this was perfectly true—all the English
nobility had vowed to support the throne—King
Arthur didn't argue. Instead, he asked the dwarf,

"Could you give us directions, then? We lost our way in the storm."

"Where were you going?" asked Spinagras.

"To look for Merlin the Enchanter."

Spinagras shook his head. "Waste of time. Merlin's not in England."

King Arthur's face fell. "Are you sure? I had heard that an enchanter was in that area, and I thought it might be Merlin."

"It wasn't, though, and he's gone now anyway. You might as well just go home, O king."

The king lowered his eyes and stared gloomily at the ground. He had convinced himself that if he could just talk to Merlin, he'd know how to save Sir Gawain from the Green Knight. Now that hope was gone. He was silent for a long time.

At last he looked up at the dwarf. "Then, can you give us directions back home to Camelot?"

Spinagras pursed his lips. "These woods are tricky. I'd better show you the way myself."

"Thank you, Spinagras," the king said dully.

"You're welcome," said the dwarf softly. "Trust me, sire. I'll see you home safe. All of you."

CHAPTER 4
Gologras's Castle

The idea of "vows" has already figured several times in this story, and since that idea is about to be important, it is worth pausing over it for a moment. A vow, of course, is a promise, but in King Arthur's time, promises meant rather more than they sometimes have since then. In the dangerous days before Arthur united England under one king, lawless scoundrels and cowardly bullies called "recreant knights" roamed the land. They did whatever they felt like doing and took whatever they wanted from anyone who was weaker than they were, for there was no one to stop them. People couldn't call the police, because there were no police, so they turned to one another for protection, making solemn vows to join together and help each other out whenever one was in need. People took these promises very seriously, because keeping their vows was a matter of life and death.

Later, when King Arthur rose to the throne, he established the Round Table and began sending his knights out to protect people from recreants and scoundrels. Life began to get better, but promises remained just as important. All the king's knights took solemn vows to help the helpless and protect the weak, and—as Spinagras pointed out— all England's nobles took vows to support the king and obey his laws and help him to bring peace.

One could say that the king's peace—indeed, the kingdom itself—was built on people keeping their promises. This was why Sir Gawain intended to meet the Green Knight, even though it meant his death; he had made a vow, and in those days a person who didn't keep his word might as well be dead anyway.

(Things are different nowadays. Nations are not founded on keeping promises so much as on bleak and gloomy things called economies, which expect people to do whatever suits them rather than what they've said they would do. Of course, there *are* still people who believe that keeping their word is a life-and-death matter; they're just less common. One should always be on the lookout for such people; they make the best friends. In fact, they make the only friends. But back to the story.)

As Spinagras said, the forest where they had

gotten lost was tricky. He led King Arthur's party through snowy woods and icy plains, over frozen lakes, and between towering crags where tons of snow hung dangerously over the path. On the first night, they made camp a hundred yards back from a small river, and rose with the sun the next morning to continue their journey.

The first to climb from his tent in the morning was Sir Reynold, who had a bump on his head just like the one on Sir Gandefere's, and who hadn't slept well on account of rolling over on the sore spot. "Odds bodikins!" gasped Sir Reynold. "Will you look at that?"

King Arthur and his knights crawled from their tents and stood beside Sir Reynold, staring down a long slope at what they had taken to be a river, but which the morning sun revealed to be a moat around a magnificent castle. "Spinagras?" called King Arthur.

"Yes, Your Highness?"

"What is this?"

"That's the castle of Sir Gologras, the wealthiest and most powerful noble in these parts."

"Gologras?" repeated the king. "I've never heard of him. How can that be, if he's such a powerful lord?"

"Gologras doesn't get out much," Spinagras said.

"But I'm the *king!* Every noble in the land swears a vow of loyalty to me!"

"Oh, right," Spinagras said. "That's why you've never met Sir Gologras. He doesn't do that."

"Doesn't do *what?*" the king demanded, his face growing stormy.

"Swear oaths of loyalty. He doesn't swear oaths at all, actually."

"*And—why—not?*" King Arthur asked through gritted teeth.

"I'm not sure. Personal preference, I imagine," the dwarf replied casually.

King Arthur looked for a moment as if he were

about to explode. "LOYALTY TO THE KING IS NOT A MATTER OF PER-SONAL PREFERENCE!" he roared.

Many of the king's knights began to edge away. They had never seen King Arthur  look quite so angry, or so purple. Spinagras only looked thoughtful. "Hmm," he said. "I wonder if any-one's explained that to Gologras."

King Arthur stared at the dwarf, speechless, for a moment, then turned on his heel and walked a good distance from the camp. His knights watched him pace and grumble and growl and take many long, deep breaths and then pace some more and, finally, plunge his head into a snowdrift for several seconds. When he returned to the others, his face was much less purple and quite a bit more damp, but he seemed to be in control of himself. "We'll make camp here," he announced. "After breakfast, we will hold council on what to do about this fellow Gologras."

At the council an hour later, Sir Gandefere advised immediate, drastic action: "Attack at once, I say!" Most of the other knights agreed.

King Arthur nodded. "I'll admit that was my first thought, too. We can't allow one noble to decide not to be part of the kingdom. If we do, then *everyone* who has a grievance or who gets tired of paying taxes will do the same. Our peace will fall apart, and we'll be right back to the bad old days of civil war and recreant knights everywhere."

"So what are we waiting for?" Sir Reynold demanded. "The fellow will swear loyalty soon enough with a sword at his neck."

"I wonder, though," mused the king, "if such an oath would really mean anything."

Sir Gawain cleared his throat. He was sitting beside Spinagras, and couldn't help remembering how promptly the dwarf had given them food when he was asked politely. "You could try talking to him first," Sir Gawain suggested. "Like Spinagras said, maybe no one's explained matters to Sir Gologras."

King Arthur looked at Gawain for a long moment, then nodded slowly. "Yes, perhaps we should do that," he said.

"Well, I think it's a waste of time," grumbled Sir Gandefere, "but if that's what you want, I can go talk to him."

King Arthur looked at Sir Gawain and Sir Gawain at King Arthur. Then both looked at their feet.

"Er, that's very kind of you, Gandefere," King

Arthur said, "but you've already done so much. Perhaps someone else could—"

"If you don't want Gandefere," interrupted Sir Reynold, "let me do it. I'll just go cut myself a cudgel to take along. No one's going to sneak up behind me this time."

"Ah, yes, a cudgel," King Arthur said. "Now, perhaps we should think about that."

"What's to think about?"

King Arthur hesitated, so Sir Gawain said, "Don't you think that taking a club along might give the wrong impression?"

"You think a spear would be better? A battle axe?"

"Gawain, you go," said King Arthur. "Speak to this Sir Gologras. Ask him why he won't swear loyalty to his king. Just *ask* for now, all right?"

"Yes, sire," said Sir Gawain.

CHAPTER 5
Sir Gologras the Unconquered

When Sir Gawain arrived at the castle and met Sir Gologras himself, he knew that King Arthur had been right not to send Sir Gandefere or Sir Reynold—with or without clubs. Officially, Sir Gologras might have been a rebel against the crown, but he was the most courteous rebel Sir Gawain had ever met. Indeed, he was the most courteous *anything* Sir Gawain had ever met.

Sir Gologras greeted Sir Gawain with pleasure and led him to a comfortable parlor, warmed by a roaring fire, where he refused to let Sir Gawain talk business until he had been given a warm drink, a plate of biscuits, and some fur-lined slippers for his feet. Sir Gawain hesitated over the slippers. It wasn't that they weren't comfortable. They were. But Sir Gawain couldn't help feeling they looked odd with his armor. At last, though, Sir Gawain was allowed to speak.

"I come as an envoy from King Arthur," he began. "The king has heard that you refuse to swear loyalty to him and to his kingdom."

"Yes, that's true," Sir Gologras said, nodding.

"Er, it is?" Sir Gawain hadn't expected his host to admit his rebellion so frankly.

"But it's not just King Arthur, you know. Your king mustn't take it personally. I don't swear allegiance to anyone."

"You don't?" asked Sir Gawain. "Why not?"

"Family tradition," Sir Gologras explained. "My great-grandfather swore an oath to a neighboring lord once. They promised to protect each other in case of danger. But when danger came, my great-grandfather's neighbor broke his vow, joined the enemy, burned my great-grandfather's home to the ground, and stole everything he had. My family's worked very hard to rebuild since that disaster, and we've done quite well, I think, but we've never again trusted someone else with our promises or let anyone else make a promise to us."

"But you *can* trust King Arthur, you know," Sir Gawain assured him.

Sir Gologras smiled politely and said, "Do you care for any more sweet breads?"

"No, thank you," Sir Gawain replied. "Look here, Sir Gologras. I'm very sorry that your great-grandfather had a bad experience with a solemn vow, but really, that isn't King Arthur's fault. And you must consider this: What would happen if everyone followed your example?"

"You mean if everyone worked hard and minded their own business?"

That hadn't been exactly what Sir Gawain meant. "Don't you see that without a king to keep order, some people—I mean recreant knights and so on—would choose to go about robbing and stealing and behaving very badly, the way it was before?"

Sir Gologras nodded sympathetically. "Too true. I've met people like that myself. But still—I have the family tradition to uphold."

Sir Gawain sighed sadly. He rather liked this knight. "Then I'm afraid I have to tell you that King Arthur is determined to make you swear loyalty to him, even if he has to use force. I wish you would reconsider; I wouldn't want you to get hurt."

"Oh, I doubt I'll get hurt," Sir Gologras said. "I'm quite a good fighter. In fact, I've never lost a battle. In these parts, they call me Sir Gologras the Unconquered."

Sir Gawain's mouth dropped open. "Seriously? Because it's the same with me. They call me Sir Gawain the Undefeated."

"You don't say!" Sir Gologras exclaimed. "Tell me—don't you find it a nuisance?"

"A . . . a nuisance?"

"You know, all those people who step out of your way when you walk by and simper and fawn over you because they're afraid you'll hurt them. That sort of nonsense."

Sir Gawain frowned. He had always rather enjoyed all that, but when Sir Gologras described it, it sounded very silly. "I hadn't really thought about it," he admitted.

Sir Gologras smiled sadly. "Tell me, Sir Gawain. How many friends do you have?"

"Dozens, I suppose. Everyone at court."

"And how many would still be your friends if you were Sir Gawain the Easily Defeated?"

Sir Gawain considered this for a long time. At last he said, "Well, there's King Arthur."

"You're lucky," Sir Gologras said. "When I ask myself that question, I can't think of even one." Sir Gologras rose to his feet. "I suppose you need to take my reply back to your king."

Sir Gawain stood, too, but he didn't move. He was still thinking about what Sir Gologras had said, about having no friends, and it seemed very sad to him. On impulse, Sir Gawain said, "Sir Gologras, I would like to be your friend. Conquered or Unconquered. Would that be all right?"

Sir Gologras blinked several times with surprise, then peered closely at Sir Gawain. His eyes held an odd expression—half amazement and half regret—but he only held out his hand. "I think I'd like that, Sir Gawain."

Sir Gawain shook his hand, then turned away to return to King Arthur. "Wait!" said Sir Gologras. "I won't go back on my family tradition, and King Arthur seems determined to make me do so, but I'd hate to go to war with my only friend. Let's see if we can avoid it. Why don't you suggest to the king that we have a single combat? I'll send one of my knights out to meet one of his knights tomorrow morning at sunrise, and we'll let their contest decide our differences."

Sir Gawain nodded. The decision-by-single-combat idea was an ancient tradition, seldom used by that time, but if the king agreed, it might prevent bloodshed. Sir Gawain left Sir Gologras, rode across the drawbridge to where the king was waiting, and delivered his message.

"Don't do it," counseled several of his knights. "We already have him outnumbered."

"Perhaps," said the king. "But he's in a castle, and we're out here. Laying siege to a fortress like this is no simple matter. If he has enough food in there, we could be camped out here for months. And a single combat *would* save lives."

"I think that's what Sir Gologras was hoping, too," Sir Gawain said. "But isn't there another way to—?"

But before he could finish, King Arthur was already calling out for the heralds to signal his acceptance of the plan.

Sir Gawain sighed and dismounted. He was glad there would not be a full-scale war, but even a single combat seemed somehow wrong to him. Then he noticed that the king and his knights were staring at him curiously. "What's the matter?" asked Sir Gawain.

"What are those?" King Arthur asked, looking at Sir Gawain's feet.

Sir Gawain looked down at his feet, still wearing Sir Gologras's furry slippers. "A gift from a friend," he replied.

CHAPTER 6

A Fairly Useless Tournament

All Arthur's knights seemed excited about the single combat the next day. It was just like a tournament, but with an actual purpose and a real prize. A buzz of eager anticipation swept through the camp, but Sir Gawain wanted none of it. He still felt that fighting Sir Gologras was a mistake, but no one else shared his misgivings. He looked for Spinagras, hoping that the dwarf—not being a knight—would understand his doubts, but Spinagras was nowhere to be found.

At the council that night, King Arthur explained to his knights what everyone had already heard by rumor: that at dawn the next day one champion from the king's camp would face one knight from Sir Gologras. If King Arthur's champion won, then Sir Gologras would swear allegiance to the throne. If Sir Gologras's champion won, then the king would leave him in peace.

Sir Gandefere the Nearly Undefeated leaped to his feet. "Sire, I request the honor of this battle for myself!"

King Arthur hesitated, glancing at Sir Gawain. "Er, I had thought—"

"I shall overcome him!" Sir Gandefere promised. "I am nearly undefeated, after all!"

"Well, see, that's the thing," King Arthur began. "Perhaps it would be best if—"

"I think Sir Gandefere would be an excellent choice, sire," Sir Gawain said quietly.

The king blinked. "You don't think it would be better for *you* to—"

"I find that I do not wish to fight Sir Gologras's knight, Your Highness."

There was a long silence as all King Arthur's companions stared at Sir Gawain. They had never heard him say such a thing before. Then the king closed his eyes and nodded. "Of course. Forgive me, Gawain. In my preoccupation with Sir Gologras's rebellion, I had forgotten that you have other things on your mind."

Sir Gawain realized that the king was talking about his upcoming meeting with the Green Knight. Oddly enough, Sir Gawain had almost forgotten about that, but he didn't correct the king's mistake. The king could think whatever he wanted, so long as Sir Gawain didn't have to fight the next day.

So it was decided that Sir Gandefere would represent King Arthur the next morning, and the knights dispersed to their tents to rest before the big day. They were all awake and dressed before dawn, and at the exact moment that the sun showed at the horizon, the great drawbridge lowered from the castle, and a knight on horseback trotted across to the field.

"I am Sir Goliot the Practically Unconquered, champion of Sir Gologras. Who challenges me?"

Sir Gandefere was mounted and waiting. "I am Sir Gandefere the Nearly Undefeated, champion of King Arthur, and I challenge you!"

Without another word, the two knights spurred their horses, lowered their lances, and charged at each other. All the onlookers held their breath, watching. The two mighty warriors came together with a tremendous crash. Both lances splintered into thousands of pieces; both knights were thrown abruptly from their horses; both landed with solid thuds on the turf. Neither moved.

For several seconds, the watchers remained still. Sir Gawain shook his head slowly, then heard a soft chuckle at his side. Glancing over he saw Spinagras, who had appeared suddenly. "Well, wasn't that useful?" commented the dwarf.

A knight appeared at the castle gate and began approaching the prone forms of the champions. King Arthur called for Sir Reynold. "Go check on Gandefere, will you?"

A minute later, Sir Reynold and the knight from the castle had determined that both knights were alive, just knocked out. "What happens now, I wonder?" Sir Gawain muttered to Spinagras. He didn't have to wonder long. Sir Reynold drew his sword and called out in a ringing voice, "I, Sir Reynold the Brave, will take the place of my fallen companion, Sir Gandefere!"

At once, the knight from the castle drew his own sword and replied, "And I, Sir Regal the Dauntless, will fight for Sir Goliot!" Then the two knights charged each other on foot, swinging their swords. They hacked and slashed and parried for a moment, backed away, then charged again.

"Shouldn't someone drag Goliot and Gandefere out of the way?" mused Spinagras. "They're rather underfoot."

For several minutes, Sir Reynold and Sir Regal fought, dancing nimbly around their unconscious companions. Then Sir Regal directed a mighty overhand blow at Sir Reynold. Sir Reynold parried the blow with his own blade, and neither was hurt, but both swords broke at the impact. For a moment, the two knights stared at their blade-less sword hilts; then both drew daggers from their belts and began slashing and stabbing and fighting with the small blades. But daggers aren't designed for cutting through armor. Ten minutes later, both knives were broken.

Sir Reynold and Sir Regal looked lost for a moment. Then Sir Reynold grasped the edge of his shield and swung it at Sir Regal. Taken by surprise, Sir Regal stumbled backward, tripping over either Goliot or Gandefere. He was up again in a trice, though, bellowing with rage and wielding his own shield as a weapon. For quite a little while, then, they bashed each other with their shields. At last, Sir Regal managed to knock Sir Reynold's shield from his grasp and, stooping quickly, Sir Regal picked it up and threw it like a discus into the castle's moat. Unfortunately, he had forgotten to put down his own shield before throwing, with the result that both shields splashed and sank into the murky water. The two knights watched until the last bubbles had disappeared, then turned to look at each other.

"Take that!" shouted Sir Reynold, throwing a

heavy punch at Sir Regal's head. "Owww!" he screamed as his fist bounced harmlessly from Sir Regal's helmet.

Sensing an advantage, Sir Regal replied at once with his own punch. "Ouch!" Sir Regal shouted, holding his hand. Fists aren't designed for penetrating armor, either.

The two knights circled each other for a moment, rubbing their bruised hands. Sir Gawain leaned close to Spinagras. "Tell me the truth, friend," he said. "Is all this, um, a little bit stupid?"

Then Sir Regal seemed to have an idea. Dashing down to the moat, he took up a stone from the water's edge and threw it at Sir Reynold. It bounced harmlessly off Sir Reynold's shoulder. "Hey!" shouted Sir Reynold. Running to the moat he found his own stone and flung it at Sir Regal, but it missed because Sir Regal had already stooped to find another rock. Sir Reynold ran

close and kicked water into Sir Regal's face, blind-
ing him. Sir Regal lost the rock he had been about
to take up, but he scooped up a handful of sand

and gravel and threw it at Sir Reynold. It made a
tinkling noise on the iron armor.

"Stupid?" replied Spinagras. "Maybe a little bit."

Now both knights were on their knees throwing gravel at each other with both hands as fast

as they could. Sir Gawain closed his eyes. "Some-one please make it stop," he moaned.

King Arthur must have been thinking the same thing, because at that moment he strode onto the tournament field and called out firmly, "Enough! Both of you!" The two knights stopped splashing and throwing dirt. "This is no way to settle a dispute!" snapped the king.

Spinagras snorted softly and muttered, almost too quietly to hear, "But hitting someone with a sword *is?*"

Sir Regal spoke, his voice sulky. "All right, then. We'll have another go at it tomorrow, but this time my master, Sir Gologras, will come himself to fight, and Sir Gologras has never been defeated!"

"Wait!" said Sir Reynold. "We may end this today, after all! Look!" He pointed at Sir Gandefere and Sir Goliot. Both had wakened and were slowly picking themselves up. They shook their heads groggily and looked around. Then they saw each other, let out a bellow of rage in unison, drew their swords as one, and bashed each other on the helmets. Both dropped to the ground like stones and lay there unmoving.

"Never mind," said Sir Reynold.

"Until tomorrow, then!" snapped Sir Regal. "You shall see what true knightly power is when you face Sir Gologras the Unconquered!"

CHAPTER 7
Sir Gawain the Once Defeated

As soon as it became known that Sir Gologras would be representing himself the next day, then Sir Gawain knew he was going to have to fight. Who could King Arthur send to face Sir Gologras the Unconquered but Sir Gawain the Undefeated? Still, Sir Gawain tried to argue.

"But, sire, I don't *want* to fight him," he explained. "I like Sir Gologras."

"I understand, Gawain," the king replied, "but this is for the kingdom. If the people of Britain are ever to live in safety, then all must agree to support one ruler. If I let Sir Gologras refuse to swear loyalty, how can I expect the rest of the people to be true?"

Sir Gawain sighed. "I know. But isn't there anyone else?"

At this moment, King Arthur received some surprising support. Spinagras the dwarf had seemed scornful of the day's tournament, but now he spoke up in favor of the next day's battle. "You must send someone, Your Highness, but don't even think about sending anyone but Sir Gawain. Speaking as one who's seen Sir Gologras fight, I can tell you that only your very best knight stands a chance. He's a demon with a sword, he is."

Sir Gawain frowned at Spinagras, but the dwarf ignored him. King Arthur looked grim, but he only said, "I'm sorry, Gawain. But it has to be you. Be ready at dawn tomorrow."

"Yes, sire," said Sir Gawain, and true to his word, he was.

As on the day before, the great castle's draw-bridge began to lower just at the crack of dawn, and when it was down, an armed and armored knight rode across to the field beyond. The knight raised his lance in salute. "I am Sir Gologras the Unconquered, here to defend my home and my family tradition. Where is your champion, King Arthur?"

Sir Gawain rode forward, stopping just in front of Sir Gologras and raising the visor on his helmet. "Here I am. Sir Gawain."

"Sir Gawain?" repeated Sir Gologras. Sir Gawain nodded. "So," said Sir Gologras, "this is your idea of friendship, is it?"

"I vowed obedience to my king, who has sent me. I will keep my vow."

Sir Gologras snorted. "See what comes of all this vow-taking business?"

"We wouldn't have to do this if you would take one yourself," Sir Gawain suggested. "Just promise never to rebel against the king. It isn't so hard."

"I have only made one solemn promise in my life," Sir Gologras said.

Sir Gawain brightened. "You have? You've made one? Then why not make just one more?"

"Because that solemn promise was to my father, on his deathbed. I promised not to make any more solemn promises."

"Well, that's not fair!" exclaimed Sir Gawain. "No, really! *Promise me not to make any promises?* That's cheating! Either you make promises, or you don't!"

Sir Gologras hesitated. "When you put it that way, it *does* seem a little irregular. But all the same, do you want me to break that promise?"

Now Sir Gawain hesitated. "No, I guess not. Just as I won't break my promise to King Arthur." He sighed. "So where does that leave us?"

"I think we have to fight," Sir Gologras said.

"Bother," replied Sir Gawain. Then they separated, rode to their positions, pointed their lances, and charged. As had happened the day before with Sir Gandefere and Sir Goliot, both knights' lances splintered, and both knights were thrown from their horses. This time, though, the two knights rose at once and continued the contest with swords.

As has already been mentioned, detailed accounts of battles are curiously dull to read. To do a fight justice, each attacking sword blow and defending parry must be noted. The problem is that the blow and parry together only take a fraction of a second, but it takes much longer than that to read about them. As a result, the poor readers get left behind. By the time they've finished with that first exchange, the knights have already gone on to have three or even four more. After that, there's no catching up at all, but only falling further and further behind, and so readers lose interest. The same sort of thing happens at school sometimes.

So, to make a long (and dull) battle story short: The swift and skillful swordplay of Sir Gawain and Sir Gologras was splendid to watch, and all who were privileged to witness their battle knew that they would never again behold such brilliant knightly warriors. The champions went on without slackening their pace for nearly an hour, but after that they slowed down slightly. They would fight a bit, then back away and circle each other, catching their breath and watching for an opening. During one of these circling times, Sir Gologras said, "I can see why you're undefeated, my friend. You really are a splendid swordsman."

"You, too," Sir Gawain replied, with feeling. "It's an honor to see such skill. After this is all over, you must show me that trick you have of twisting your blade at the parry to drive my sword further off course. I've never seen anything like that."

"Do you like it? I came up with that myself."

"You've nearly had me a dozen times with that trick," Sir Gawain said.

"And what about the way you switch hands?" commented Sir Gologras. "That took me completely by surprise the first time you did it. Do you practice as much with your left hand as with your right?"

"More, actually," Sir Gawain said.

"Amazing," replied Sir Gologras. "We must train together after this."

"Unless one of us is dead."

The two knights circled in silence for a moment.

"Yes," Sir Gologras said at last. "Unless one of us is dead."

They closed again and fought fiercely and brilliantly for several minutes. They each landed several blows on each other, but only on the places that were best protected by their armor. Then they broke apart to circle again.

"I thought you had me there for a moment," said Sir Gologras as soon as he had his breath. "When

I slipped just then, I left quite an opening at my neck. I'm surprised you didn't cut off my head."

"I . . . ah . . . I thought it might be a trap," Sir Gawain said. "And what about you? When I lunged forward and you stepped aside, you could have brought your sword right down on my back, where my armor's weakest."

Sir Gologras said nothing for a long moment. At last he murmured, "I . . . thought it might be a trap?"

They circled some more.

"This is going to go on for a long time, isn't it?" asked Sir Gawain.

Sir Gologras nodded. "And yet it can't end until one of us wins. When it's over, one of us will no longer be unvanquished."

"Does that really matter so much?" asked Sir Gawain.

"That, my friend, is a very good question," replied Sir Gologras slowly. "Ready to go again?"

"Ready," said Sir Gawain.

They charged again, and once more the swords flickered and swung and clanged and thudded. The watchers in the field and on the castle walls could scarcely see the blades, so swiftly did they move, but the knights themselves always seemed able to block each thrust or slash. Then Sir Gawain got his chance. Sir Gologras swung a mighty blow, which Sir Gawain parried, but the force of the two swords striking was such that Sir Gawain's right hand went numb. Realizing that Sir Gologras's sword hand might also be numb, Sir Gawain quickly switched his blade to his left hand and brought the hilt down on Sir Gologras's hand. It worked. Already numb, Sir Gologras lost his grip on his sword. Sir Gawain stepped on it, then laid the edge of his own blade on Sir Gologras's neck.

"Yield, Sir Gologras," he said.

Slowly, Sir Gologras sank to his knees and re-moved his helmet. "I can't yield," he said.

"What?"

"If I yield, then I'll have to swear loyalty to the king, and I've promised not to do that."

"Then what do we do?"

"You won, Sir Gawain. You'll have to kill me now."

"I don't *want* to."

"Nevertheless, you have to. Go on. Cut off my head."

"Blister it! Why do people keep asking me to cut off their heads?" exclaimed Sir Gawain, furiously. "I don't *like* cutting off heads!"

"Well, I don't see what else we can do."

Sir Gawain glared at his stubborn friend for a long moment. Then he said, "Unless this is one of your traps."

"Eh?"

"You could be kneeling in order to take advantage of me. You know that my right hand is numb and probably can't hold my sword very tightly."

"You're holding your sword in your left hand," Sir Gologras pointed out.

Sir Gawain shifted his sword back to his right hand. "As I was *saying*," he continued, "you could be planning to knock my own sword out of my hand, then shove me back off your sword and get the advantage."

"Seems like a pretty stupid trap to me," said Sir Gologras.

"That's what makes it such a good plan. No one would suspect it. You'd take me completely by surprise."

"Would I?"

"Yes."

With one hand, Sir Gologras knocked Sir Gawain's sword from his grasp. With the other he pushed Sir Gawain a step backwards. Grasping his own sword, Sir Gologras rose to his feet and laid the blade on Sir Gawain's neck. "Yield, Sir Gawain."

"I do yield," replied Sir Gawain. "Gladly."

A minute later, both knights stood before King Arthur, who looked grim. "You have won, Sir Gologras," he said. "And I will keep my word and leave you alone now. You may refuse to swear an oath of allegiance, whatever the consequences to the kingdom may be."

Sir Gologras shook his head. "I may have won, but Sir Gawain has proven himself the better man. Sire, I am not able to swear a solemn oath of loyalty to you. To do so would mean breaking an earlier promise. But would you accept my word as a friend?"

"Am I your friend?" asked the king mildly.

"Not yet, but my friend Gawain vouches for

you, so I'd like to be. And I don't take up arms against friends. I've done it once now, and I've decided not to do it again."

King Arthur considered this. "That isn't a solemn vow, though. Is it?"

"No, it isn't. It's just what I say. But you may trust it."

The king smiled. "All right. That's good enough for me. In the end, I'd rather have the word of a friend any day."

Slowly, all the knights began to realize that the whole matter had been resolved, without any bloodshed or any broken promises, and all rejoiced. Sir Gawain grinned happily at Sir Gologras. "Well, you certainly took me by surprise, friend."

"Not half so much as you've surprised me," replied Sir Gologras.

CHAPTER 8
Saying Goodbye

The king's party stayed several more days at Sir Gologras's castle, enjoying themselves very much. Sir Gandefere and Sir Goliot became fast friends, and after big meals were often to be found side by side on adjacent armchairs, sharing a nap. (Sir Reynold and Sir Regal never did really hit it off, though.) At the end of a week, the royal caravan set out for Camelot. As Sir Gawain took his leave of Sir Gologras, his friend smiled broadly and said, "Do not say goodbye. We are friends now. I look forward to many years of good times together. I'm sure I shall see you again soon."

Sir Gawain smiled automatically, but said nothing. He had not told Sir Gologras about the Green Knight and the beheading trial that he was to face on New Year's Day. He didn't want to distress his friend. Sir Gologras pointed them in the right direction, and the knights of the Round Table set off for home.

They had gone hardly a mile when a new rider approached the cavalcade, and Sir Gawain was pleased to recognize Spinagras the dwarf. "Well, where in the world have you been, Spinagras?" he called out. "I haven't seen you since the day of the useless tournament."

"I had some business to take care of back home—I told you I was a steward, didn't I? Yes, I

thought I had. And besides, I thought you'd be killed and didn't want to see it. But here you are, alive and well. Did you really beat the great Sir Gologras?"

"Oh, no," Sir Gawain replied. "I was defeated, but he spared my life. Then he and Arthur made friends, which is better than making promises, so everything worked out in the end. Why have you come back now?"

"I thought that King Arthur might need a guide to Camelot."

"How did you know we were leaving today?" Sir Gawain asked, curiously.

"Lucky guess, I suppose," Spinagras replied airily. "So do you know how to get where you're going?"

"Sir Gologras pointed us southwest."

"Hmm," said the dwarf. "That's right, but you'll still need someone to show you the best places to cross rivers and all that. I'd better ride along."

"That's kind of you," Sir Gawain murmured.

"Not at all," Spinagras said. "I enjoy showing people the way to go. It's what I do best."

Sir Gawain thought about this for a moment. "So you must know England pretty well."

"Better than any map," Spinagras said promptly.

"I don't suppose you know a place called the Green Chapel, do you?"

Now it was Spinagras's turn to be silent, but after a moment he said, "Yes, I know it. Why do you ask?"

"I need to go there in a year on New Year's Day," Sir Gawain replied.

"I wouldn't do that if I were you," Spinagras said bluntly. "It's an eerie place, not pleasant at all. I could show you a lovely beach near Brighton, if you like."

"All the same, I have to go there. I took a vow."

"See what comes of all this vow-making business," Spinagras muttered under his breath. Sir Gawain looked at him curiously, but Spinagras only said, "Yes, I'll take you there. I won't go to it myself, mind you, but I'll take you near enough that you can't miss it."

Spinagras led the king and his knights to Camelot, then disappeared again, and for the ensuing months, life went on very much as normal in the court. The only thing, really, that disturbed the pleasant Camelot routine over the next year was the fact that every now and then people would remember that when winter came Sir Gawain would be riding away to die. The court still held the usual balls and banquets, but Sir Gawain stopped attending them, because he could see that his presence put a damper on the festivities. Sir Gawain began taking long rides, just to get away, and twice tried to go visit Sir

Gologras, but without Spinagras to show him the way, he never could find his friend's castle, and no matter where he looked or who he asked, no one else seemed to know where to find it.

On Christmas Eve, when Sir Gawain had just eight days to live (he tried not to keep count, but it was impossible not to), the castle gates opened to admit a visitor, and Spinagras the dwarf rode into the central court. Sir Gawain was almost relieved to see his guide, even if he *was* coming to guide him to the Green Knight. Things had gotten very bad at court. For weeks now, ladies had been bursting into tears at the mere sight of him, which was very distressing. Sir Gawain never had figured out what to do with a weeping lady.

Sir Gawain said his goodbyes that evening, and the next morning he and Spinagras left before dawn. As soon as they were past the castle gates, Sir Gawain asked the dwarf, "I say, Spinagras, will

this journey take all week? Because I'd really love
to stop by and see Gologras on the way."

Spinagras looked at Sir Gawain for a long moment. His eyes were hard to read, though Sir
Gawain thought he saw sympathy in them. But
he only said, "Sorry. The road to the Green Chapel
is hard going. If we don't go straight there, we'll
never make it by New Year's."

Sir Gawain sighed. "Then will you take Golo-gras a message from me? Tell him I really wish we'd had more time together."

"You sound as if you'll never see him again," the dwarf said.

"I won't," Sir Gawain replied. He didn't try to explain, and Spinagras didn't ask.

Spinagras had been right about the difficulty of the road. They climbed over harsh crags and rode across frozen, windswept moors. They pushed heavily through dense forests, crept delicately across treacherous frozen lakes and marshes, and ploughed shoulder-deep through thick snowdrifts. At last, two days before the new year, as they made camp in a little hollow out of the wind, Spinagras said, "We're almost there, Sir Gawain. Tomorrow morning, if you ride to the top of that hill over there, you'll see the castle of Sir Bred-baddle the Huntsman. He can take you the rest of the way."

"Where will you be?" asked Sir Gawain.

"I told you last winter. I won't go to the Green Chapel myself. It's not a healthy place. But don't worry. Sir Bredbaddle may not be the cleverest fellow in creation, but he can get you where you need to go."

Sir Gawain thanked the dwarf, and they both rolled over in their blankets by the fire. When Sir Gawain awoke the next morning, Spinagras was gone.

CHAPTER 9
Sir Bredbaddle the Huntsman

As Spinagras had promised, Sir Gawain saw the castle as soon as he came to the top of the hill. Riding toward it, he tried to remember the name of the knight who lived there—Bottleberry? Budpuddle? something odd, anyway—but as it happened he didn't have to remember at all. As soon as he approached the gates, the drawbridge lowered and a man rushed out, calling "Yoohoo! Yoohoo! Over here!"

This man wore the strangest-looking clothes he had ever seen. Mostly green, his breeches and doublet had patches of brown and black sewn onto them in apparently random patterns. Sir Gawain raised his hand in greeting and started to speak, but the man was already talking.

"My name is Sir Bredbaddle the Huntsman. Do you know why they call me the huntsman?"

"Er, because you like to hunt?"

Sir Bredbaddle looked crestfallen. "Did someone tell you?"

"No, it was just a lucky guess," Sir Gawain said hurriedly. "I am Sir Gawain."

Sir Bredbaddle's mouth dropped open. "Sir Gawain the Undefeated?"

"Not anymore, I'm afraid," Sir Gawain said.

Sir Bredbaddle blinked. "You're not Sir Gawain anymore?"

"No, I'm . . . I'm still Sir Gawain. I'm just not undefeated anymore."

"Oh!" exclaimed Sir Bredbaddle. "Why not?"

"Because I . . . I got defeated," Sir Gawain explained.

"Oh, right. That would do it, wouldn't it? Well, never mind. You're still welcome in my castle. We don't get many visitors out here, so we can't be choosy." Sir Bredbaddle smiled reassuringly. "Why, we've sometimes entertained knights who have been defeated *several* times."

"Very generous of you, I'm sure."

"Oh, think nothing of it. As I say, it gets lonely out here on the moors. Will you come in? How long can you stay? A week? A month?"

"Only one night, I'm afraid. Tomorrow, on New Year's Day, I have to meet someone at the Green Chapel, which I understand is nearby."

"The Green Chapel? Oh, ay, that's three furlongs from here. But the knight who lives there is a great nasty wizardly sort. I shouldn't go if I were you."

"Nevertheless, I must."

"Suit yourself," Sir Bredbaddle said, waving his hand. "Let's go in by the fire. Aggie! Aggie! Look what I have! I have a guest! You'll never guess who it is! Aggie!"

As Sir Bredbaddle led Sir Gawain down the hall, Sir Gawain asked, "Who is Aggie?"

"My wife! Here she is!"

They entered a firelit parlor, and Sir Gawain stared at Sir Bredbaddle's wife, a beautiful woman in a golden gown gathered at her waist with a green sash. Sir Gawain knew her at once. She was the lady he had rescued from the dragon more than a year before. He bowed courteously and started to speak, but once again Sir Bredbaddle was too fast for him.

"Aggie, this is Sir Gawain the Defeated. Make him comfortable by the fire. I'll go tell the cook to toss another bird in the pot for dinner." With that, Sir Bredbaddle disappeared down a corridor.

Sir Gawain looked at the lady. "My lady, I am very glad to see you again."

"Are you?" she asked softly.

"I am. I'm afraid I was very rude to you that day when I fought the dragon. I never even asked your name."

"I am Lady Agnes."

"Oh, good. I was hoping you weren't really named Aggie."

Lady Agnes smiled. "That's only what my husband calls me."

Sir Gawain bowed again. "Then, Lady Agnes, may I beg your forgiveness for treating you so indifferently that day in the forest? I am deeply sorry."

Before Lady Agnes could reply, Sir Bredbaddle breezed back into the room. "The cook says he'll be glad to cook up another meal, but since I left you, I've had an even better idea! What do you say we provide our own dinner?"

"I beg your pardon?" asked Sir Gawain, puzzled.

"Go hunting, of course! I was just about to go out anyway, when I saw you approaching. That's why I'm in my hunting clothes! Do you like them? I designed them myself. They're all green, but with different colors, just like the colors of the woods. When I wear them you can hardly see me, because I look just like the forest. I've even invented a special name for these clothes."

Feeling that he was supposed to ask, Sir Gawain said, "What name is that?"

"I call them *clothes that when I wear them you can hardly see me, because I look just like the forest.* So what do you say? Would you like to go hunting with me? I'm a very good huntsman, you know. I'm sure we'll bag something delicious for dinner."

Sir Gawain bowed his head politely. "I thank you very much for your invitation, Sir Bredbaddle, but if you don't mind, I think I would rather not. I've been riding for many days in the open, and now that I've finally arrived at my destination, I'd rather not go back out in the cold."

Sir Bredbaddle looked crestfallen. "Are you sure? Because there's really nothing to do around here."

"Doing nothing sounds very nice, actually."

"Very well," Sir Bredbaddle said with a sigh. "Shall I stay and keep you company? Aggie hardly talks at all, so if I go hunting, you'll be stuck here in horrible quietness."

"No, Sir Bredbaddle," Sir Gawain said hastily. "Please don't change your plans on my account. I beg you: go ahead and hunt."

"But what about you, all quiet and still here by the fire? Won't it be dreadful?"

"I shall try to bear it bravely," Sir Gawain assured him.

Sir Bredbaddle shook his head with consternation. "I just don't understand! A knight is always striving, seeking, hunting! I know how it'll be! I'll leave you here, and in an hour you'll be hunting around for something to do . . ." Sir Bredbaddle's eyes lit up. "And I'll prove it to you! We'll have a game! I'll go hunting in the forest, and whatever I take in my hunt I'll give to you at the end of the day. You stay here, and whatever you get inside, you give to me! I'll wager you'll have nothing to show for your day! What do you say? Is it a game? Or, if you'd rather, I could stay and chat with you all day."

"It sounds like a wonderful game!" Sir Gawain said quickly. "You should go on to the hunting field at once!"

Sir Bredbaddle grasped Sir Gawain's hand and shook it vigorously. "Fine! Now, remember! Give me all you get! I'm taking it as a solemn vow!" With that, he hurried from the room.

Sir Gawain and Lady Agnes stood in silence for

nearly a minute, listening to the slowly fading noise of Sir Bredbaddle's shouting voice. At last, Lady Agnes said, "When my husband came in just now, you were apologizing to me, were you not?"

"I was," replied Sir Gawain. "Can you forgive me?"

Lady Agnes gave him a speculative look. "I will admit that I was quite angry with you for some time after that day. You saved my life from the creature, but then you spoke only of yourself, refused to let me give you any token of thanks, and then rode off leaving me to find my own way home. I might have died there, and I did spend rather a lot of time imagining ways to punish you for your selfishness."

Sir Gawain waited in silence.

Lady Agnes continued. "But, yes, since you ask, I shall forgive you. Nevertheless, you must allow me to give you the tokens of thanks that I offered you before."

"Whatever you wish, my lady," Sir Gawain said humbly. "I am yours to command."

Lady Agnes stepped forward. "First, a kiss." She stood on her tiptoes before Sir Gawain and gave him a quick peck on the cheek. "Thank you for saving my life, Sir Gawain." Then she untied the

green sash that was around her waist. "And second, this sash. I tried to tell you a year ago, but you interrupted me. This is a magical sash, woven by my mother, the Enchantress Agostes, and the knight who wears it can never be harmed by any weapon. Please take it as a token of my gratitude." She placed the sash in his hand, smiled, then left the room.

Sir Gawain stared at the sash, open-mouthed. There in his hand lay life. With that sash, he would be able to survive the next day. The Green Knight's axe would not harm him. He could return to Arthur's court. He could see his friends again. He could live.

The rest of the day was like a dream to Sir Gawain. All the misery of the past months had faded away, and he spent hours in blissful peace, making plans for the future. Then, just as the sun was lowering in the sky, he heard a bang from the courtyard and a loud shout. Sir Gawain recognized Sir Bredbaddle's voice and strolled out to greet his jovial host. The huntsman stood proudly in the middle of the court, showing off a magnificent stag that he had felled.

"Look at this fellow, why don't you? Don't you wish you had gone hunting with me? It was a grand day!" Sir Gawain smiled and said nothing. Then Sir Bredbaddle said, "But I remember our bargain! This stag is yours. Now your turn! Give me everything *you* got today!"

CHAPTER 10
Sir Gawain the True

Sir Gawain's heart stood still. Not once that day, basking pleasantly in the gift of life that he had received with Lady Agnes's sash, had he thought about Sir Bredbaddle's silly game. Why had he agreed to such a thing? To get rid of the irritating Sir Bredbaddle, of course. How could he have known that making such a promise would lead to this? Maybe Gologras (and Spinagras, too) had been right about the foolishness of making vows. But the vow had been made. Now, to keep his casual promise, he had to surrender the sash and face certain death. His mind reeled, but in the midst of the whirl was one idea: *A vow is a vow*. In a daze, he stepped forward and gave Sir Bredbaddle a dutiful kiss on the cheek. Then he reached for the green sash at his waist.

But Sir Bredbaddle gave him no time. He was roaring with laughter. "Oho!" he shouted gleefully, "Now I know why you stayed behind! Been hunting chambermaids, haven't you? Well, well, we all have our different specialties!" He clapped Sir Gawain heavily on the back, laughed again, then led him into the castle, exclaiming loudly, "But I won in one way, didn't I? All I had to give away was a deer, while you—you had to give me a kiss! Well, that's the price you pay, I suppose. See what comes of all that vow-making business?"

Slowly, Sir Gawain turned and stared at Sir Bredbaddle, an impossible idea taking shape in his mind. *It couldn't be.* Sir Bredbaddle glanced back at him, and Sir Gawain quickly assumed a polite expression, even as his mind, suddenly clear, raced ahead, putting things together. "Yes, of course," Sir Gawain said with a smile. "You're quite right. Tell me about your hunt. Was it a difficult chase?"

Now, as Sir Gawain well knew, nothing is more gratifying to an outdoorsman than to be allowed to describe every minute of a good day in the field, and Sir Bredbaddle talked without ceasing for two hours before dinner, for another two hours during the grand venison feast that they shared that evening, and then for two hours after eating. Sir Gawain smiled and responded with polite interest and heard hardly two words. His mind was occupied with plans. He no longer had any intention of returning the green sash—at least not yet—but when? And how? He thought about it all through supper and went to bed still pondering the question, but when he awoke before dawn, he knew exactly what to do. He rose, dressed, folded the green sash carefully, and tucked it in his pocket. Leaving his weapons and armor in his room, he went out into the corridor to go knock at Sir Bredbaddle's door.

As he'd expected, he was prevented from doing so. As soon as he left his chamber, a servant approached. "Good morning, Sir Gawain," said the servant. "I was just coming to wake you."

"You were?"

"Yes, my master says you have to go to the Green Chapel today, and if you're going to the Green Chapel, you have to go at dawn."

"At dawn? Why?"

"Those are the rules of the chapel, Sir Gawain. Are you ready?"

"Isn't Sir Bredbaddle going to take me himself?"

"My master never arises early."

Sir Gawain smiled to himself and played along. "But I haven't had a chance to thank him for his hospitality. Surely it would be all right to wake him."

"Besides," said the servant hastily, "it's a holiday. My master always sleeps in on holidays. He's very particular about such things."

Sir Gawain knew the servant would never take him to Sir Bredbaddle's room, and why, so he allowed the servant to hurry him down to the courtyard, where his horse was saddled and waiting. "You must leave at once," the servant said. "Go out the main gate, take the path to the left, and stay on it. It will lead you directly to the Green Chapel." The gates of the castle opened, the servant slapped Sir Gawain's horse on the haunches, and the steed leaped into a run.

As the servant had promised, the path led

straight to the chapel. The sun was just peeking above the horizon when Sir Gawain rode into a clearing. It was an ancient and eerie-looking place, where the grass waved as fresh and green as if it were the first of June instead of the first of January. In the center of the clearing stood a round low structure with cavelike openings instead of doors. From behind that, Sir Gawain heard the raspy sound of an axe being sharpened on a stone. He rode around the chapel. There stood the Green Knight from the Christmas feast, his head back on his shoulders and looking, if anything, even taller than he had the year before.

"Ah, there you are, Sir Gawain!" called the knight. He tested the edge of his blade with his thumb and nodded with satisfaction. "I'm glad to see you. Some people don't keep their promises, you know."

Sir Gawain ignored these words, scanning the

wild knight's face for anything that looked familiar. He saw nothing, but Sir Gawain was sure he was right.

"What's the matter, Sir Gawain?"

"Excuse me for staring," murmured Sir Gawain, dismounting. Beside the whetstone stood a thick old oak stump, scarred and crossed with many axe cuts. Sir Gawain made his way toward this stump.

"You're not wearing your armor," the Green Knight said.

"No," replied Sir Gawain, "these are the clothes that I wear when I know I won't need to fight. I have a special name for them, in fact."

The Green Knight raised one eyebrow. "And what would that be?" he asked.

"I call them my *clothes that I wear when I know I won't need to fight*," Sir Gawain explained innocently.

The Green Knight's eyes narrowed, and they held a suspicious light as they examined Sir Gawain. Sir Gawain tried to keep his face blank and turned back to the stump. "Is this where you chop off heads?" he asked.

"It is."

"Well, that's why we're here, isn't it? Let's get on with it." He knelt at the stump, then glanced up. "Go ahead, then. Chop off my head."

The Green Knight didn't move.

"Well?" demanded Sir Gawain, assuming an air of impatience. "Come on, then. I haven't got all day. I mean that, you know. I *really* haven't got all day—just one part of it. So chop off my head, why don't you?"

Still the Green Knight didn't move. "No one has ever actually *invited* me to chop off his head," he muttered.

"They haven't?" asked Sir Gawain. "It happens

to me all the time. First you, last New Year's, then a dwarf named Spinagras, then a knight named Gologras. Annoying, isn't it?"

"A little," the Green Knight admitted.

Smiling to himself, Sir Gawain bowed his head at the stump again. The Green Knight cleared his throat and stepped forward, and Sir Gawain held up his hand. "Oh, just one thing before you swing." Digging in his pocket, he produced the green sash that Lady Agnes had given him the day before and tossed it to the Green Knight. "You didn't give me a chance to give this to you last night, but here's one more thing I got from my day in your castle: your wife gave it to me."

The Green Knight froze, and Sir Gawain turned around and grinned. The Green Knight lowered his axe. "How did you figure it out?"

"Lucky guess, I suppose," replied Sir Gawain. "It was all a test, wasn't it? I behaved like a scaly cad to your wife that day in the forest, so you set up this whole beheading game to punish me."

"It was something like that," the Green Knight replied.

"Yes, she mentioned that she had spent some time plotting revenge."

"Not revenge, exactly," the Green Knight said, "just a little lesson in manners. And if I may say so, you've been an excellent student. Agnes says you are now the most courteous knight she's ever met."

"By the way," Sir Gawain asked, "how do you change shape like that?"

"I'm not just a knight. I'm a sorcerer, too, on my father's side. I'm particularly good at shape shifting."

"Yes, you are," Sir Gawain agreed. He took a deep breath, then turned around again. "Well, are you going to cut off my head now?"

"Well, no, I wasn't planning on it," replied the Green Knight.

"But a vow's a vow," Sir Gawain said sternly.

"You may have vowed to let me hit you—a vow you've kept, by the way—but if you'll think back, you recall that I never made any vow at all."

"Ah, yes," Sir Gawain said, nodding. "After all, you promised your father you wouldn't make any vows, didn't you?"

The Green Knight's mouth dropped open. "You've even figured *that* out?"

"That was the part I figured out first. It was something you said. So tell me, which do you prefer to be called? The Green Knight? Bredbaddle? Gologras? Or Spinagras?"

The Green Knight smiled broadly, then began to chuckle, then to laugh. As he laughed, his green coloring faded and his features rearranged themselves until he was in Sir Gologras's shape.

"I like best to be called your friend," the knight said. "Come on, I believe Agnes should have our breakfast ready by now."

King Arthur never stopped telling his knights that courtesy was as important as courage, even if his knights didn't always quite see what he was getting at. But after that year, Sir Gawain at least never forgot it. He remained the most courtly, most courteous, most honorable of all the knights of the Round Table—and, above all, the best and most thoughtful of companions. No one called him Sir Gawain the Undefeated any longer. Indeed, most forgot that he had ever been called such a thing. People called him Sir Gawain the True, unless they were lucky enough to be one of those who could call him, simply, "friend."